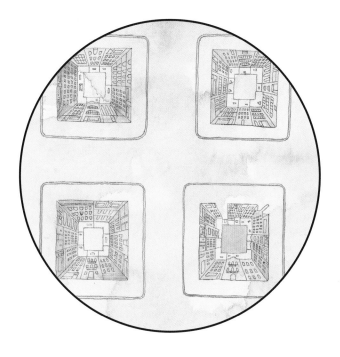

For my team, FSG

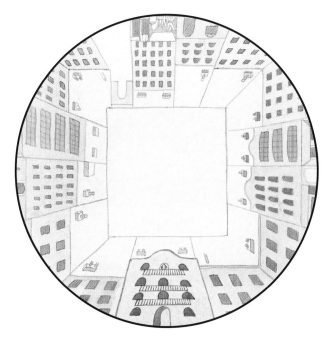

Copyright © 2010 by Peter Sís
All rights reserved
Distributed in Canada by D&M Publishers, Inc.
Color separations by Chroma Graphics
Printed in June 2010 in China by South China Printing Co. Ltd.,
Dongguan City, Guangdong Province
Designed by Natalie Zanecchia and Robbin Gourley
First edition, 2010
1 3 5 7 9 10 8 6 4 2

www.fsgkidsbooks.com

Library of Congress Cataloging-in-Publication Data
Sís, Peter, date.
    Madlenka soccer star / Peter Sís. — 1st ed.
        p.   cm.
    Summary: Madlenka plays soccer in her city neighborhood—with the mailbox,
a dog, a parking meter, and some cats.
    ISBN: 978-0-374-34702-4
    [1. Soccer—Fiction.   2. Imagination—Fiction.   3. City and town life—Fiction.]   I. Title.

PZ7.S6219Madb 2010
[E]—dc22
                                                    2010005498

MADLENKA SOCCER STAR

PETER SÍS

FRANCES FOSTER BOOKS

Farrar Straus Giroux · New York

In the universe, on a planet, on a continent, in a country, in a city, on a block, in a house, lives a little girl named Madlenka,

who dreams of being a soccer star.

Here comes Madlenka out the door

with her brand-new soccer ball.

She dribbles it around the corner
on her way to the courtyard.

Madlenka has lots of friends on the block,
so there's always someone to play with.

And everyone wants to play soccer.

But the mailbox isn't fast enough.

Oh, there may be a fight for the ball here.

But Madlenka heads it off . . .

. . . and keeps on going.

Nothing can stop her.

But who will she play with now?

Do cats like soccer?

YES!

But they can't beat Madlenka.

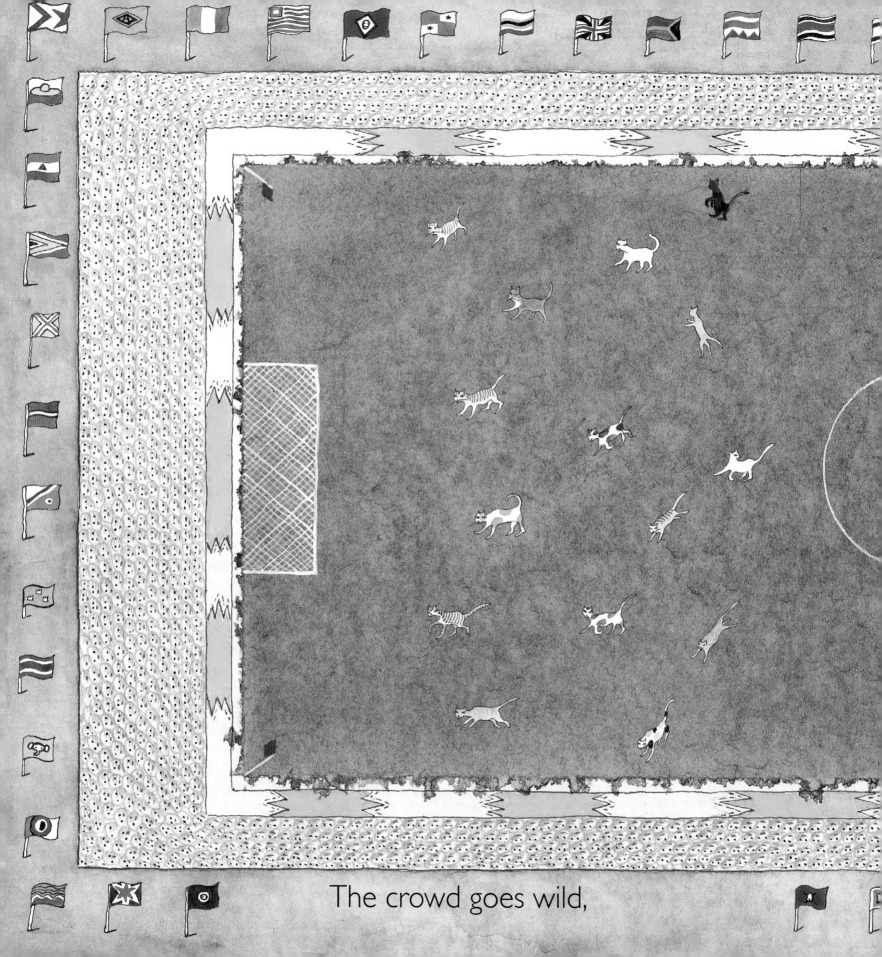

The crowd goes wild,